'Be careful,' Anne said. 'He's a very good painter, but he's a very bad man.' Every woman in the room watched Rory Balniel. We all wanted him.

Emily knows that a bad man is what she wants. So when she meets Rory Balniel, the exciting, beautiful painter, there isn't any question. No other man is right for her. But how bad is he?

When she is his wife, she meets Marina – the beautiful Marina – and she thinks she knows. But there is worse, much worse, to come . . .

Jilly Cooper is one of Britain's best-known writers, and is often on radio and television. She was born in 1937 in Yorkshire, England. Her first jobs after she left school were on small newspapers, and she had many other jobs before she started writing books. *Emily* (1975) was the first of her stories and now her books sell more and more every time. Her last three books, *Riders*, *Rivals* and *Polo* were all number one bestsellers. *Riders* was a television film in 1993. She often writes about rich men and women and their exciting lives.

Now Jilly Cooper lives in Gloucestershire with her family, and her dogs and cats. She writes in a summer house at the bottom of her garden.

OTHER TITLES IN THE SERIES

Level 1
Girl Meets Boy
The Hen and the Bull
The Medal of Brigadier Gerard

Level 2
The Birds
Chocky
Don't Look Now
The Fox
The Ghost of Genny Castle
Grandad's Eleven
The Lady in the Lake
Money to Burn
Persuasion
The Railway Children
The Room in the Tower and Other Ghost Stories
Simply Suspense
Treasure Island
Under the Greenwood Tree

Level 3
Black Beauty
The Black Cat and Other Stories
The Book of Heroic Failures
A Catskill Eagle
Channel Runner
The Darling Buds of May
Dubliners
Earthdark
Jane Eyre
King Solomon's Mines
Madame Doubtfire
The Man with Two Shadows and Other Ghost Stories
More Heroic Failures
Mrs Dalloway
My Family and Other Animals
Rain Man
The Reluctant Queen
Sherlock Holmes and the Mystery of Boscombe Pool
The Thirty-nine Steps
Time Bird
Twice Shy

Level 4
The Boys from Brazil
The Breathing Method
The Danger
Detective Work
The Doll's House and Other Stories
Dracula
Far from the Madding Crowd
Farewell, My Lovely
Glitz
Gone with the Wind, Part 1
Gone with the Wind, Part 2
The House of Stairs
The Locked Room and Other Horror Stories
The Mill on the Floss
The Mosquito Coast
The Picture of Dorian Gray
Strangers on a Train
White Fang

Level 5
The Baby Party and Other Stories
The Body
The Firm
The Grass is Singing
Jude the Obscure
The Old Jest
The Pelican Brief
Pride and Prejudice
Prime Suspect
A Twist in the Tale
The Warden
Web

Level 6
The Edge
The Long Goodbye
Misery
Mrs Packletide's Tiger and Other Stories
The Moonstone
Presumed Innocent
A Tale of Two Cities
The Thorn Birds
Wuthering Heights

Emily

JILLY COOPER

Level 2

Retold by Michael Nation
Series Editor: Derek Strange

PENGUIN BOOKS

PENGUIN BOOKS

Published by the Penguin Group
Penguin Books Ltd, 27 Wrights Lane, London W8 5TZ, England
Penguin Books USA Inc., 375 Hudson Street, New York, New York 10014, USA
Penguin Books Australia Ltd, Ringwood, Victoria, Australia
Penguin Books Canada Ltd, 10 Alcorn Avenue, Toronto, Ontario, Canada M4V 3B2
Penguin Books (NZ) Ltd, 182–190 Wairau Road, Auckland 10, New Zealand

Penguin Books Ltd, Registered Offices: Harmondsworth, Middlesex, England

First published by Arlington Books (Publishers) Ltd 1975
This adaptation published by Penguin Books 1995
3 5 7 9 10 8 6 4 2

Illustrations by Bob Harvey

Typeset by Datix International Limited, Bungay, Suffolk
Printed in England by Clays Ltd, St Ives plc
Set in 11/14 pt Monophoto Bembo

To the teacher:

In addition to all the language forms of Level One, which are used again at this level of the series, the main verb forms and tenses used at Level Two are:

- common irregular forms of past simple verbs, *going to* (for prediction and to state intention) and common phrasal verbs
- modal verbs: *will* and *won't* (to express willingness) and *must* (to express obligation or necessity).

Also used are:

- adverbs: irregular adverbs of manner, further adverbs of place and time
- prepositions: of movement, further prepositions and prepositional phrases of place and time
- adjectives: comparison of similars (*as . . . as*) and of dissimilars (*-er than, the . . . -est in/of, more* and *most . . .*)
- conjunctions: *so* (consequences), *because* (reasons), *before/after/when* (for sequencing)
- indirect speech (statements).

Specific attention is paid to vocabulary development in the Vocabulary Work exercises at the end of the book. These exercises are aimed at training students to enlarge their vocabulary systematically through intelligent reading and effective use of a dictionary.

To the student:

Dictionary Words:

- Some words in this book are in darker ink than the others. Look them up in your dictionary or try to understand them without a dictionary first, and then look them up later.

CHAPTER ONE

I only went to Annie Richmond's **party** because my friend Nina asked me to go again and again.

'But I can't go without Cedric,' I told her. 'I'm going to **marry** Cedric soon.'

'So where is he, Emily?' Nina asked.

'He's working,' I said.

'Again! I don't know why you love him. You never go out now, you don't see your friends . . .'

I thought about one more evening at home without Cedric. Then I started thinking about men . . . and whisky . . . and **sex**.

'No!' I said. 'I'm not going to Annie's party. It's wrong.'

So an hour later I went. That's me.

There were a lot of people at Annie's party. I liked it. I had a drink, and then a very nice man in a red shirt started to talk to me. I told him about Cedric and he went away, so I didn't talk about Cedric again. Then the room went quiet and the sexiest man in the world walked in. He was tall with long, black hair, dark, smokey eyes and a strong mouth – a beautiful animal.

'Annie, who's that?' I asked.

'Rory Balniel,' she said. 'He's a **painter** and very rich. He lives on an **island** in the west of Scotland.'

'I must talk to him,' I said.

'Be careful,' Annie said. 'He's a very good painter, but he's a very bad man.'

Every woman in the room watched Rory Balniel hungrily. We all wanted him. A pretty girl talked to him for a few minutes and then he started to open her dress.

Then the room went quiet and the sexiest man in the world walked in. 'I'm Rory,' he said and kissed my hand.

'Stop it,' the girl shouted.

The man in the red shirt walked up to Rory. 'Stop that, Balniel. You can see she doesn't like it.'

Rory pushed the girl away, then he broke a bottle on a table and pushed it at the man's face. 'I do what I want!' he shouted angrily.

Nobody could like Rory Balniel – but I knew that I wanted him. He saw me and came over to me.

'What's your name?' he asked.

He was so strong and exciting. My legs went weak.

'Em— Emily,' I said.

'I'm Rory,' he said and **kissed** my hand.

'Oh, Cedric,' I said weakly.

'Who's Cedric?' Rory asked and kissed my hair.

'I'm going to marry him,' I said.

'Are you?' Rory kissed my ear.

'It's very hot in here,' I said. 'My dress is too hot.'

'Let's go to your place and take it off, then,' Rory said.

'Oh no, I can't do that.'

So we went home and took off my dress.

CHAPTER TWO

The next morning I stayed in bed and looked at Rory next to me. Suddenly he opened his eyes and looked at his watch.

'Oh no! It's ten-thirty!' he said. 'I'm meeting somebody at eleven.'

Rory put on his clothes, said, 'See you,' and left.

I waited for him to phone me, but he didn't, then at six o'clock he came back. He looked very ill.

'Did you have a good meeting?' I asked.

'What? Oh, yes. I'm going to have a big **exhibition** next spring,' he said. 'I'm ill, Emily. Can I stay here?'

Rory went to bed and slept for hours. The next day he was better. He pulled me into his arms, and into bed.

'Rory! Stop it. You're ill! Oh, oh, Rory . . .'

Two hours later Rory said, 'Marry me, Emily.'

'Marry you?' I asked. He could marry any woman in the world. 'But . . . but. . .' Then he kissed me, and I couldn't think of anything when he kissed me.

The telephone went and Rory took it.

'Hello,' Rory said. 'Ah, Cedric! My name's Rory Balniel . . . Yes, that's right . . . I'm in bed with Emily . . . Yes, in bed . . . And I'm going to marry her, Cedric, so please don't phone again. OK?' He put the phone down. 'Is that Cedric?' Rory looked at the photograph next to the telephone.

'It was,' I said and smiled. 'I'm going to marry you, Rory.'

'Bye bye, Cedric,' Rory said and threw the photo out of the window.

CHAPTER THREE

Nina thought I was **mad** to marry Rory.

'He never stays with a woman for more than five minutes,' she said. 'And how can you live on an island?'

I didn't think about that, I was too happy. I wore a beautiful hat when we got married, but Rory threw it into the street when he saw it.

'Don't wear a hat again,' he said. 'I want to see your hair.'

That night we went to Paris. Rory had a lot of whisky to drink at our hotel. He was very excited and I was afraid of him. Later I put on some **perfume**, got into bed and waited

I wore a beautiful hat when we got married, but Rory threw it into the street when he saw it.

. . . and waited. Then I heard Rory speaking on the phone in the other room.

'I'm in Paris,' he said. 'Remember Paris? I'm married now, the same as you!' He put the phone down.

'Who was that, Rory?' I asked.

He was very angry. 'Don't ask me questions!' he **shouted**. 'Never ask me questions!' Then he took me in his arms and kissed me madly all over.

In Paris I started to know Rory. One minute he was happy, the next minute he was sad, and the next minute he was angry. I loved him, but it was very difficult.

CHAPTER FOUR

One afternoon we were in bed, when someone came to the door. Rory opened it and said, 'Oh hello, Mother. This is my wife, Emily. Emily, meet my mother.'

I had nothing on, nothing but a smile. 'Oh, he— hello, I . . .' I said.

Rory's mother kissed me and said 'Hello Emily, I'm Coco. Rory, she's very pretty!'

Coco was beautiful. She wore a lot of **make-up** and perfume, and a very expensive Dior dress.

'Where's Buster?' Rory asked.

'Buying an aeroplane,' Coco said, and smiled at me. 'Buster's my second husband, Emily. Hector, Rory's father, is dead now.'

'How did you know we were here, Mother?' Rory asked.

'Marina told me,' Coco said. 'And you didn't!'

'Marina?' Rory said coldly. 'How's her old husband?'

Suddenly Buster walked in. He said 'Hello' to me and smiled. He was younger than Coco.

Suddenly Buster walked in. He said 'Hello' to me and smiled. He was younger than Coco.

'Did you buy your aeroplane, Buster?' Rory asked.

'Yes,' he said. 'And Finn McClean is going to get an aeroplane, too.'

'Who's Finn?' I asked.

'Marina's brother,' Coco said. 'He's the doctor on the island, and he's building a hospital.'

'I don't like him,' Rory said. 'You two can go away now. Emily wants more sex.'

CHAPTER FIVE

After two weeks in Paris we went to my new home, the island of Irasa, in the west of Scotland. It was cold, the sky was dark, and through heavy rain I saw an old **castle**.

'Coco and Buster live there,' Rory said. 'This is our house, next to the castle.'

It was a nice house, but it was very dirty inside. I looked out of the bedroom window. The sea was a hundred metres below.

'Oh,' I said, 'somebody's left flowers for us on the bed.'

But they were flowers for the dead, and I read the words 'Now you're home!' on the paper.

'Oh no. Rory, who did this?'

'I don't know.' Rory said. He threw the flowers out of the window and down they went, down into the cold sea. Suddenly I heard a car drive fast along the road past the house, a blue car. The driver was a girl with red hair, and she looked in at us with sad, hungry eyes.

CHAPTER SIX

A woman came to clean the house and do all the cooking. I loved to walk round Irasa and look at the trees and the small

They were flowers for the dead, and I read the words 'Now you're home!' on the paper.

white houses. One day in the town of Penlorren the girl in the blue car drove past again, very fast.

'There's Marina Buchanan,' an old woman said to her friend. 'Mad girl!' Then they saw me and walked away quickly.

My **marriage** was not happy. Rory did not kiss me and he was often angry, but I didn't know why.

'I love you, Rory,' I told him. 'Do you love me?'

'No,' he said. 'You're not good in bed.'

'But, but . . . Rory, you didn't tell me,' I said.

He laughed. 'Because I'm not interested in you!'

Rory went out in his car. I ran to my bedroom and cried for hours. Then I heard somebody at the door. It was Marina Buchanan. She was very tall and beautiful. She had big, dark eyes, and her long red hair moved slowly in the wind.

'I'm Marina . . .'

'I know,' I said quickly. 'Come in. Have a drink.'

We drank whisky and talked a lot.

'My husband's very rich. I only want his money. He isn't very interesting.' Marina said. 'Where's Rory?'

'He went out,' I said.

'Is he being difficult?' Marina asked.

'No!'

'Oh, don't be angry,' she said. 'I know Rory's a difficult man, but he's very sexy, too.'

'Marina,' I said suddenly, 'come to dinner on Thursday. Bring Hamish.'

Rory came in. 'Hello,' he said to me. He didn't look at Marina.

Marina laughed. 'Really, Rory, say hello to me!'

Rory kissed me hard on the mouth, then he said coldly, 'Hello, Mrs Buchanan. How's Mr Buchanan?' but he didn't want to look at her.

Rory said coldly, 'Hello, Mrs Buchanan. How's Mr Buchanan?' but he didn't want to look at her.

CHAPTER SEVEN

Marina and Hamish came to dinner. She was very beautiful and he wasn't. Rory and Marina laughed at him.

'I think he looks younger in his white shirt and trousers,' Marina said.

'Yes, he does. Not eighty years old, only seventy,' Rory said.

After dinner Marina said, 'Rory, can I see the painting you're doing now?' and they went to his painting room.

Hamish sat next to me and tried to kiss me, so I went to talk to Rory and Marina. The painting room was dark but I saw Rory and Marina in there. She stood near to him.

'Why did you marry her?' Marina asked in a quiet voice.

'Because you didn't marry me,' Rory said.

'I don't love Hamish,' Marina said. 'But Emily is young and pretty. Do you love her, Rory?'

He didn't answer. She started to cry, and ran out of the room. She didn't see me. Her face was wet with crying. She and Hamish went home.

'Rory!' I shouted. 'What's happening? You spoke to Marina on the phone that night in Paris. I know it now! And she left those flowers on the bed. I know that, too!'

'Marina is one of my oldest friends. We were children together on this island,' Rory said. 'And you asked her to dinner, not me.'

'Why is she always looking at you?' I asked. 'Why is she always talking about you?'

He didn't answer. 'I'm going to bed now,' he said coldly. 'And I'm going to sleep in a different bedroom. I don't want you tonight.'

Why is she always looking at you?' I asked.
'Why is she always talking about you?'

I took Rory's arm. He pushed me away and I hit one of the big tables in the room. A lot of paintings came off the table and went all over the floor. They were all paintings of Marina. Marina with no clothes on, Marina with her long red hair over her face and her body.

'Oh, Rory. Why did you marry me?' I asked.

'I don't know,' he said.

'Oh, Rory, try to love me. Please.'

'I want to paint,' he said. 'That's all I want.'

'Well, I want more!' I shouted. 'Much more!'

We slept in different rooms that night and for weeks after that. I thought about Marina and I cried. Then I thought about Rory, and I knew I loved only him, and could never stop.

CHAPTER EIGHT

Marina and Hamish asked us to dinner in November. A **good-looking** man called Calen was there.

'You're very beautiful,' Calen said after dinner, and sat next to me. 'Can I kiss you, Emily?'

'No. Stop it, Calen,' I said. 'I was only married seven weeks ago.'

'Oh, a very long time,' Calen said. 'Come on, let's kiss.'

I must say, I liked it, and Rory didn't kiss me.

Later, when we drove home Rory said, 'I see you found a new friend to play with. Calen's a child, too!' And he laughed.

♦

The next week Coco broke her leg. I went to Penlorren to buy her a book before I went to see her at the castle. When I

'You're very beautiful,' Calen said after dinner, and sat next to me. 'Can I kiss you, Emily?'

came back to my car I saw a big, strong man with red hair there.

'Is this your car?' he asked me angrily.

'Yes,' I said.

'Can you read?' he asked me. 'Look at that.'

I saw the words DOCTOR'S CAR – NO STOPPING on the garage door behind my car. So this was Finn McClean.

'Move your car now!' he shouted. 'I must go. People are dying because of you!'

'No, they aren't,' I said. 'I'm going, I'm going!'

'Move!' he shouted.

Finn McClean was as mad as his sister. I got into my car and called him lots of bad names – but quietly, he was a very big man. Then I drove to the castle.

Coco was in bed. 'Have a drink, Emily,' she said. 'And give me a drink, too.'

We talked for some time and then Coco's doctor walked into the room – Finn McClean!

'Ah, Finn,' Coco said. 'This is Emily, Rory's wife.'

'Oh,' he said, and looked at me coldly. 'Now I understand.'

'Oh? Understand what?' I asked.

'You're as bad as your husband,' Finn said. 'How are you, Coco?'

I didn't like Finn McClean.

CHAPTER NINE

In December one of Coco's friends, Maisie Downleesh, gave a big party for her daughter's birthday.

'I'm going to look very beautiful for Rory,' I thought. 'And he's going to love me again after this party.'

'Move your car now!' Finn shouted. 'I must go. People are dying because of you!'

I went to Edinburgh alone and bought a sexy new dress, new shoes and perfume. Then I went to a very expensive shop where they washed my hair and put it up nicely for me. I was there for a long time. When I arrived at Downleesh castle, Rory looked at my hair.

'I don't like that,' he said.

Before the party I put on my new dress and perfume, and a lot of make-up. I looked at Rory dressed all in black, and thought that he was the sexiest man in the world, the same as the first night I saw him.

Calen was at the party. He looked at my hair and dress. 'You look beautiful,' he said and kissed me. 'Mmm, I like your perfume.'

'Rory never does that,' I thought.

I looked at Rory. His face went red and a light came into his eyes. Only Marina did that to him. She came into the room with Hamish behind her. Finn and a pretty young woman were with them.

'Hello, Doctor,' Rory said coldly to Finn. 'Is that your wife?'

'No,' the young woman said. 'I work with Doctor McClean.'

'Oh yes, work.' Rory said. 'Now I understand why your wife left you, Finn, because of your work!'

'Are you trying to paint again, Rory?' Finn asked.

'Rory's a very good painter,' I said. 'He's going to have an exhibition in London in April.'

'Do you pay Emily to say that, Rory?' Finn asked. 'Or does she say it because you love her and are so good to her?'

Rory couldn't think of an answer to that, and he was very angry.

People started to dance and I had a good time trying all the

I looked at Rory. His face went red and a light came into his eyes.
Only Marina did that to him.

Scottish dances. I danced with Calen, and then we went for a walk to look at the castle. One of the rooms was dark and Calen took me in his arms and kissed me.

'Calen,' somebody behind us said, 'you're wanted on the telephone.' It was Finn McClean.

'Not now,' Calen said.

'It's your wife, Calen,' Finn said.

After Calen left us Finn said, 'Do you think kissing Calen is going to help your marriage?'

'Help?' I laughed. 'Help? Oh, this is all wrong, Finn. I'm here in an old castle, there's dancing, beautiful flowers, perfume. Look at my hair, my dress. It's all for Rory. But where's my husband, Finn? Where *is* he? You know, but you can't say it. He's with your sister!'

'No,' Finn said quickly. 'No. They're not in love!'

'I think they are.' I said.

'You drank too much whisky this evening, Emily,' Finn said. 'Go to bed.'

I went to my bedroom and went to sleep very quickly. Rory came to bed hours later.

'Were you with Marina?' I asked him.

'She left with Hamish at eleven o'clock,' he said.

'Rory,' I said. 'Rory, I . . .' but he went to sleep. I looked at him for a long time, then he put his arms round me.

'My love,' Rory said in his sleep. 'Oh, my love.'

I cried quietly because I knew his 'love' wasn't me.

CHAPTER TEN

One day after the party I came back to the house after doing some shopping and heard Rory and Finn shouting.

'I don't want you to see Marina again!' Finn said.

'But where's my husband, Finn? Where is he? You know, but you can't say it. He's with your sister!'

'Marina can do what she wants,' Rory shouted.

'I know you two are going to start again,' Finn said.

'That's right,' Rory laughed.

Finn was very angry. 'I can go to the police about you and Marina, Rory,' he said.

'What!' Rory jumped at Finn, but Finn hit him hard on the face and suddenly Rory was on the floor.

I ran into the room and shouted, 'Stop! Stop it now!'

Finn said nothing. He looked at Rory for a minute, then he walked out of the house. Rory stood up. He walked to a table and took a bottle of whisky. He put the bottle to his mouth and drank nearly half. He didn't speak.

'Why did Finn talk about the police?' I asked. 'Rory?'

He took a gun from the table. I think he was mad. He laughed at me. 'Do you want to go to bed, Emily? Do you?'

'Rory, please!' I said. 'No!'

Suddenly he **shot** the gun at the wall. 'I told you not to ask me questions, Emily!' he shouted.

'Please! Please!' I shouted.

'Let's go to bed,' Rory said. 'I want you now, Emily. Now!'

'Rory, no! No, I don't want to!' I said. 'Stop it! Please, Rory. No!'

He pushed me down to the floor, and pulled my clothes off. When he had finished with me he started to cry. 'Emily! I'm sorry. Oh God, I'm so sorry,' he said.

CHAPTER ELEVEN

One day in February I was out on a small road near Penlorren, when my car stopped suddenly and I couldn't move it.

I ran into the room and shouted, 'Stop! Stop it now!'

Another car came very fast along the road and stopped only a metre away from my car. Finn McClean got out.

'Oh no, it's you,' he said.

'I'm sorry,' I said. 'I can't move my car.'

'Get out,' Finn said. He did something to my car and it started again. 'You see?' he said. 'It's easy.'

I don't know why but I started to cry and I couldn't stop.

'Oh, I'm sorry,' Finn said. 'Emily, I . . .'

'I'm so unhappy,' I said. 'Rory's away, I can't sleep, I'm very tired all the time, and . . .'

'Emily,' Finn said, 'I'm going across to the island of Mullin by boat this afternoon. It's very nice. Come with me.'

So I went to Mullin with Finn. The sun came out and the beaches of Mullin were white against a blue sky and blue sea. We moved quickly over the sea. Finn went to see a woman who was ill and I waited for him, then we walked over the island together.

'How's your hospital?' I asked.

'It's nearly finished,' Finn said. 'It's very exciting for me. I love working on Irasa, you see.'

He had a nice face, and I saw that he was a big man but he moved comfortably and easily.

'It's Buster's birthday party tonight. Are you coming?' I asked. 'Please try to come.'

CHAPTER TWELVE

I waited for Finn at the party, but he didn't come. Hamish asked me to dance, then he said, 'It's time you and I talked, Emily.' We went into a quiet room.

'What do you think about your husband and my wife?' Hamish asked me.

The sun came out and the beaches of Mullin were white against a blue sky and blue sea. We moved quickly over the sea.

'I don't want to talk about this,' I said.

'But you must, Emily,' Hamish said. 'I know Marina doesn't love me, and she only wants my money.'

'I don't understand that,' I said. 'Rory's as rich as you are, but Marina didn't marry him.'

'But Rory only got his father's money when he married,' Hamish said. 'He had nothing before that.'

'That's easy. He could marry Marina and get the money,' I said.

'Oh, no! Rory's father said he couldn't have the money if he married Marina,' Hamish told me.

'Rory always does what he wants, money or no money,' I said. 'But he didn't marry Marina. Why not?'

Hamish looked at me for a minute, then he said, 'Because Rory and Marina are brother and sister.'

'No!' I shouted. 'No!'

'Oh, yes,' Hamish said. 'They're half-brother and half-sister. They have the same father, Hector Balniel, but different mothers.'

'But when did Rory and Marina know this?' I asked.

'A year ago,' Hamish said. 'Rory was in love with Marina and told his father he wanted to marry her. Hector said no, and then he told Rory about Marina. Rory was very angry, nearly mad. Hector died that same night.'

'And then Marina married you, and . . . and Rory married me,' I said. 'Oh God!'

I wanted to die. I ran into the garden and I looked into the sea far below me in the dark. Then strong hands took my arms. It was Finn.

'Oh Finn,' I said, 'did you know about Rory and Marina?'

'Yes, Emily,' he said.

Finn took me in his arms and kissed me. It was warm and good.

I ran into the garden and I looked into the sea far below me in the dark. Then strong hands took my arms. It was Finn.

CHAPTER THIRTEEN

The next morning I was ill and I went to see Finn. He looked at me and later he said, 'You're going to have a baby, Emily.'

'I can't!' I said, but then I remembered that day after Buster's birthday when Rory had the gun . . . 'Rory's baby,' I said.

'Do you want to stay with him?' Finn asked.

'This is his baby. Yes, I want to stay,' I said.

'You can live with me,' Finn said.

'Oh no,' I said. 'Everything is different now.'

'I understand,' Finn said quietly. He looked very tired.

'Thank you, Finn.'

I wanted to tell Rory when I got home, but he didn't look at me when I said 'Hello' and I couldn't talk. The weeks went past and I never found the right time to tell Rory.

One day I was out walking with Coco. We looked at Finn's hospital.

'It's finished now,' Coco said. 'A new doctor's working there. She's very beautiful, and I think Finn's in love with her.'

So Finn had a new love, and I only had Rory. I drove home quickly to tell Rory about our baby.

I ran up the **stairs**. 'Rory!' I said. 'We must talk.'

I ran into the bedroom, and there they were in the bed, Rory and Marina.

♦

'I'm sorry, Emily,' Marina said, 'but it's better you know about this.'

'I knew a long time ago,' I said and ran into the bathroom. Later Rory came to the door.

'Marina went home,' he said. 'Let's talk. Open the door.'

'No!'

'Emily!' Rory said. 'Open this door.'

'Go away!' I shouted.

Rory took his gun and shot the door open. 'Come here!' he said. 'Who told you about Marina and me?'

'Hamish,' I said. 'And he says that she's your sister.'

'Oh God, Emily, I'm sorry,' Rory said. 'When I married you, I loved you, but then I came back to Irasa and I knew I was in love with Marina again. We couldn't stop it.'

'Get out!' I shouted. 'I never want to see you again!'

Two minutes later I heard Rory leave the house. I ran to the stairs. I don't know what happened next, but suddenly I couldn't stop. I was on the floor and then I went down the stairs, over and over. Then everything went black.

When I opened my eyes again it was the next day and I was in Finn's hospital. I was very tired and ill.

'We found you on the floor near the stairs,' Finn said. 'Emily, you nearly died.'

'My baby,' I said. 'What happened to my baby? Please!'

'I'm sorry, Emily,' he said. 'You lost your baby.'

I was very sad. 'Where's Rory?' I asked.

'He left the island,' Finn said. 'And I think Marina went with him.'

CHAPTER FOURTEEN

I stayed in the hospital for many days and thought about my baby. Finn came to see me every day.

'I love you, Emily,' he said.

'Tell him to leave, Finn,' I cried. 'Please tell him to go away.'

'I thought you loved your new doctor. What's her name? Jackie Barrett,' I said.

'Jackie!' Finn said and laughed. 'No.'

Then one day Rory came to the hospital. I heard him outside my door. 'I want to see Emily Balniel,' he said.

'You can't,' Dr Barrett said. 'She lost her baby and she's very ill.'

'Baby!' Rory ran into the room. 'Emily! What's this about a baby? Did you lose it?'

'Yes, Rory,' I said, sadly, 'I lost the baby.'

'But you didn't tell me about the baby – why?' Rory asked.

'Because you're in love with Marina,' I said.

'Was it my baby?' he asked.

'Oh, Rory! Go away! Go away!' I started to cry.

Finn came in. He put his arms round me.

'Tell him to leave, Finn,' I cried. 'Please tell him to go away.'

Rory left the room.

◆

Rory came back the next day.

'I'm sorry,' he said. 'Take these. Please.' He gave me some beautiful flowers.

After that he came every day, and brought me books and more flowers, and, one day, a bottle of whisky. I drank too much of the whisky that evening and when Finn came to see me I kissed him hard. He kissed me harder, and we kissed some more. Then he heard the telephone and Finn went into another room to answer it.

I danced round the room and sang, 'I love you, Finn! I l-o-o-ve you!' Suddenly I stopped. Rory was there, behind the door.

'Oh God,' I said. 'Did you see everything?'

'Yes I did,' Rory said. 'And you're coming home with me now.'

'I can't,' I said. 'I'm ill and Finn wants me to stay here. Ask him.'

But when Finn came back his face was very unhappy. 'There was a bad fire on a ship near the island,' he said. 'I must help. Emily, we want all the beds in the hospital. You're better now and you can go home.'

So Rory took me home. The house was very clean, there was a big, warm fire and a lot of flowers.

'You're my wife,' Rory said. 'I don't want you to see Finn again.'

'You go to bed with your sister,' I shouted, 'and then you tell me that I can't kiss another man!'

'Go to bed,' Rory said.

'Is Marina in it?' I shouted. He hit me on the mouth and left the room. I cried for a long time before I went to sleep that night.

CHAPTER FIFTEEN

I slept for most of the next day. At six in the evening I got out of bed and phoned Finn.

'Can you come to see me now?' I asked.

'I can't, Emily,' he said. 'I must stay here. The men from the ship are very ill.'

I didn't understand anything. Finn loved me, but he didn't come to see me. Rory loved Marina, but he wanted me at home with him.

One evening Rory said, 'My paintings for the exhibition are finished.'

Because he was happy Rory kissed me, and it all started again – fire, flowers, love. I knew Rory was the only man for me.

'I'm going to Edinburgh tomorrow,' he said.

Tomorrow was Thursday and I knew that Marina went shopping in Edinburgh every Thursday.

'Why?' I asked.

'I'm going to see a man about an exhibition in New York,' Rory said. 'I'm coming back in the evening. My mother's giving a party for her sister, Marcelle.' He kissed me again.

◆

But on Thursday morning Marina came to see me. So Rory wasn't with her in Edinburgh! I was so happy that I kissed her.

'Does Rory often talk about me?' Marina asked.

'No, not much,' I said. 'Do you love him?'

'Yes,' she said. 'And Rory loves me. He's only with you because I'm his sister, you know. Go away with Finn, Emily. He loves you.'

'Does he, Marina? I don't see him very often,' I said.

She was angry and left the house. Half an hour later Finn came to see me. He kissed me and it was very nice, the same as eating good food or listening to Mozart, but it wasn't love.

'Did you know that Rory was in Edinburgh?' I asked Finn.

'Yes, Marina told me. Come away with me, Emily, please,' he said. 'I love you.'

'No, Finn, I can't. Rory is the man for me,' I said. 'I can't go away with you. I'm sorry.'

CHAPTER SIXTEEN

Nobody was very happy that evening at Coco's party. When Coco's sister, Marcelle, arrived, everybody in the room went quiet and looked at the man with her. He was very tall and good-looking with long black hair, dark eyes and a sexy mouth. He was about fifty years old.

'Alexei!' Coco said and kissed him on the mouth.

'Ah, Coco,' he said. 'Why did you leave me?'

Coco laughed. 'Alexei was my boyfriend before I married Hector,' she said to us.

Rory walked across the room and stood in front of Alexei. He looked at him carefully. They had the same eyes, the same mouth, the same face. We could all see it.

'Mother,' Rory said. 'Tell me, is this man my father, or was Hector?'

Coco laughed. 'Oh, Rory, Alexei's your father. Yes. Are you very angry?'

'No, I'm not,' Rory said. 'But now I know why I'm very good-looking.'

Everybody laughed. Suddenly, Marina ran up to Rory, threw her arms round him and kissed him. 'Oh, Rory,' she said. 'We're not brother and sister. Everything's all right!'

◆

Rory and I stayed at the castle that night. Marina's words, 'He's only with you because I'm his sister', went round inside my head. Now Rory and Marina could get married.

'Do you like your new father?' I asked Rory in the morning.

'Yes,' he said. 'We're going to go shooting this afternoon. There's a lot of birds round the castle.'

Rory walked across the room and stood in front of Alexei. He looked at him carefully. They had the same eyes, the same mouth, the same face.

Later Finn came to see me. 'I'm going to Glasgow this afternoon,' he said. 'But I'm unhappy about Marina. She's very excited and Hamish is sad and quiet. Phone me if anything happens, please.'

At about four o'clock Rory, Buster, Hamish and Alexei went out to shoot in the trees near the castle. Later I saw Marina leave the castle and walk over to the trees where the men were. I followed her and we stood together near the men and watched them with their guns.

'I talked to Hamish last night,' Marina said sadly. 'He doesn't want to finish our marriage.'

'Good,' I said.

'Go away with Finn. Please, Emily!' she said suddenly. 'I can be with Rory then.'

'No. Never. Rory is my husband!' I shouted. '*My* husband!'

'Quiet, you two,' Buster said. 'We're going to shoot.'

All the guns shot at the same time and birds came down from the sky like rain. Then it was very quiet. The dogs went into the trees to get the dead birds and Buster went to help.

Suddenly, Buster started to shout, 'Rory! Rory! Come here quickly!'

Rory ran into the trees. When he came out his face was white.

'Hamish is dead,' he told Marina. 'Shot in the head. He did it with his new gun.'

Marina started to cry. Rory took her in his arms.

CHAPTER SEVENTEEN

I went sadly home and Rory went to help Marina. I thought our marriage was finished. Hamish was dead, so Rory and Marina could marry now. I wrote a short letter to Rory:

'Hamish is dead,' Rory told Marina. 'Shot in the head. He did it with his new gun.'

My love,
I'm going away. Be happy with Marina, and don't try to find me.
Emily

I went to London and stayed in a cheap hotel. It was spring, the trees were green and new, and the air was warm. Lovers walked in the streets, but I had nobody. Rory's exhibition opened and I read about it. Everybody said he was one of the best painters in the country. I went to the exhibition and a man there spoke to me.

'Do you want to buy one of the paintings?' he asked.

'No,' I said. 'Do you know Rory Balniel?'

'Yes,' he said, 'and he's not a nice man. His wife left him, and all this morning he stood by the door and waited for her to come. Look, that's his wife.'

The man showed me a painting. It was one of me in a blue shirt and trousers.

'It's the only painting Mr Balniel doesn't want to sell,' the man said. Suddenly he stopped and looked at me more carefully. 'My God, but it's you!'

The man told me where Rory's hotel was and I ran to find it, but there was Rory in the street, coming back to the exhibition. He took me in his arms and kissed me.

'Oh, Rory,' I said. 'I thought you loved Marina.'

'Marina wasn't right for me. I loved you all the time, Emily. I know that now,' he said. 'I tried to show you. But I thought that you loved Finn.'

'No, Rory, no! I love you!'

We laughed and then we kissed. We walked slowly along the streets of London and talked about what to do. We were so happy.

'You know,' Rory said. 'I don't want to live on Irasa.'

'Because of Marina and Finn?' I asked.

We walked slowly along the streets of London and talked about what to do. We were so happy.

'No!' Rory laughed. 'Because I want us to live somewhere warm and to have lots of children.'

'Oh, yes,' I said. 'Lots of children.'

'You know, Emily, I think Marina's in love with Alexei now,' Rory said.

'That's good. She's rich and Alexei's good-looking,' I said. Then I stopped. 'My God! Rory, if Marina marries Alexei . . .'

'Yes,' he said. 'Marina's going to be my new mother!'

EXERCISES

Vocabulary Work

Look back at the 'Dictionary Words' in this story. Do you understand them all now?

Write eight new sentences. Use *two* of these words in each sentence:

party	*painter*	*mad*	*castle*
to marry	*island*	*perfume*	*good-looking*
marriage	*to kiss*	*to shout*	*to shoot*
sex	*exhibition*	*make-up*	*stairs*

Comprehension

Chapters 1–6

1 Can you say where?

a Where did Emily first meet Rory Balniel?

b Where did Emily and Rory go that night?

c Where was Emily and Rory's new home?

Chapters 7–12

2 Who says these words? (All of the speakers are speaking to Emily.)

a 'You're very beautiful. Can I kiss you?'

b 'I'm sorry. Oh God, I'm so sorry.'

c 'I know Marina doesn't love me and she only wants my money.'

Chapters 13–17

3 What is the speaker trying to say?

a In chapter 13, Emily says to Finn: 'Everything is different now.'

b In chapter 14, Emily says to Rory: 'Is Marina in it?'

c In chapter 16, Rory says to Coco: 'Now I know why I'm very good-looking.'

4 Answer these questions.

a Why did Emily go to Annie Richmond's party without her boyfriend, Cedric?

b Why did Emily's friend, Nina, think she was mad to marry Rory?

c Why did Emily think about throwing herself into the sea after a party?

d Why did Emily lose her baby?

e Why did Emily go away to London and stay in a cheap hotel?

f Why did Rory not want to sell the painting of Emily in the exhibition?

Discussion

What do you think of the people in this story? Who is the best person and who is the worst person? Say why.

Writing

Write a story for the Irasa newspaper about how and why Hamish Buchanan died. Use about 100 words.

Review

Which chapter of the book did you like best? Why?